A Horse Named RAY-RAY

By Reed Johnson

Illustrated by Grace Metzger Forrest

A Horse Named Ray-Ray
Published By: Reed Johnson

ISBN: 978-0-578-33525-4 (Paperback Edition)
ISBN: 978-0-578-33526-1 (eBook Edition)

Library of Congress Catalog Card Number: 1-10258567081

Dedication

I have written this story for Jennifer LaDow. Without my sister's knowledge of horses and competition, writing this children's book would not have been possible.

Proceeds from this book will be used to care for my sister, who experienced a brain aneurysm in 2019. During her recovery, we would talk about her horse, Ray-Ray. These conversations were to help her regain her memory. The first place Jenn wanted to go after getting out of rehabilitation was to see Ray-Ray. In helping my sister, I came to realize that girls and their horses share an extraordinary bond.

Encouraging all girls to learn to ride will help them become better individuals. The competition these girls faced created character and maturity. This book tells a story of sportsmanship, history, teamwork, morals, and good work habits. I wrote this book with a desire to teach girls they can achieve success through time honored life lessons. Competitive Trial Riding is open to all family members over the age of ten. Take a child horseback riding today!

Thank you to my team of experts. My illustrator and editor were so very patient with the author.

Sting Ray is his real name, but we call him Ray-Ray.

"Hi, my name is Ray-Ray. I like to ride in competitive trail riding events. My partners come from all over the world to ride with me. Competitive trail riding includes navigating a series of obstacles and other special things my partner and I do. Both of us have important jobs. The judges watch us perform as a team—and as a team, we have to support each other, love each other, encourage each other, and look out for each other. Many horses like me love to ride and help girls be the best they can be. Let me introduce you to my friends."

"Jenn is my owner, and we are from America," Ray-Ray said. "Jenn and I will be riding past bleating sheep. Bleating is when sheep say, 'Bah, bah, bah.'"

"Oh, Ray-Ray," Jenn said. "I am scared of the sheep. They are trying to scare you!"

"Don't worry, Jenn," Ray-Ray said. "Be strong and believe in us. We'll make it. This test is for the judges to grade. And the sheep are not mean. They're just doing their job."

"Well, they sure are doing a great job," Jenn said. "They are making all kinds of noise."

"Bah, bah," went the last sheep, as Jenn and Ray-Ray strolled past.

"Hey, Ray-Ray," Jenn said. "What was he saying?"

"He was saying goodbye to us and that we will meet at the pasture fence later to talk about the competition. He wished us good luck, and I neighed back to him, 'Great job, Mr. Sheep.'"

Jenn smiled and patted Ray-Ray on the neck, reassuring him. She was happy the team had skillfully maneuvered the sheep, since the judges watch intently for mistakes. Receiving a high grade from the judges would not have been possible had the team not practiced many times before the competition.

Ray-Ray and Jenn

"In today's competition, my rider is from Canada," Ray-Ray said. "Her name is Charlotte."

"Ray-Ray, I think the judges are getting ready to hand me an umbrella," Charlotte said. "The umbrella is open, but I don't want you to be nervous. I will hold the umbrella away from your head and high above mine."

"I am a little nervous," Ray-Ray admitted. "But I trust you, Charlotte, because you are my teammate. I am going to stand right here and be very still, so the judges know I am not afraid."

Ray-Ray, with his big brown eyes, watched the umbrella. Charlotte held it high above her head. Ray-Ray smiled and congratulated Charlotte on a job well done.

"Thanks, Charlotte," he said. "I knew I could count on you."

Ray-Ray and Charlotte

"In today's contest, my friend, Amigo, is with his partner, Maria," Ray-Ray said. "Let's see how they do!"

"Amigo," Maria said, "I think we are going to have to walk over that black tarp. I don't know what's under it. Are you scared?"

"I don't know what's under the black tarp either, and I am a bit worried about what could happen. But I know that if we work together, we can make it across."

In this trial, the tarp was laid flat on the ground. Bricks and rocks held it in place. When there was a breeze, the tarp flapped in the wind like a flag fluttering. The team of Maria and Amigo would need to get across, and they could only do that if they worked together.

"The judges are watching," Amigo said. "Let's be cool and calm."

Maria inched Amigo forward. Amigo took a step onto the tarp and smiled.

"I can do this with your help, Maria," Amigo said.

Maria nodded. "We can do this together."

Amigo worked his way across quickly and quietly. As Amigo crossed the tarp, there was a big sigh of relief and, at the same time, a sense of accomplishment. Maria and Amigo were very proud to have made it. After all, who knew what could have been under that tarp?

Amigo and Maria

"In today's trial," said Ray-Ray, "my friend, Rosie, is with her partner, Amelia. Let's see how they do!"

"Rosie, I think we're going to have to walk through these rails," said Amelia. "I don't want to trip and fall, so let's be careful. Are you scared?"

"I don't want to trip over them either," Rosie said. "We will have to take our time, make good decisions, and we can make it."

Amelia nodded. "I agree. Making team decisions is the key to being successful, so let's do what you suggest."

In this trial, four rails are placed on the ground, ready to trip up riders. The rails are lined up vertically, and each is placed four feet apart. The team of Amelia and Rosie must walk through the rails without touching them or moving the post.

"The judges are watching," Rosie said. "Let's be cool and calm."

Amelia slowly inched Rosie forward. Rosie, working with her teammate, carefully maneuvered around and over each post.

"I am trying hard not to touch them, Amelia," Rosie said, working her way across confidently. "All we can do is do our best and put our best foot forward."

"I know you can do it!" Amelia said.

Rosie knew her teammate was looking out for her. Rosie and Amelia made it across without touching the posts. Once they were done, Rosie stood still so that Amelia could dismount.

The judges were impressed with their teamwork. They received high marks for their effort.

Rosie and Amelia

"In today's competition," Ray-Ray said, "my friend, Mozart, is with his partner, Annabella. Let's see how they do!"

"Mozart, I think we are going to have to walk past these balloons," Annabella said. "It's a windy day, and those balloons are just bouncing in the wind and all over the place. I don't want one to touch you and make you jump."

"I don't want to be unexpectedly frightened either," Mozart said. "It's like your brother jumping out from behind the door and scaring you. I know he thinks it is funny, but I saw you jump when he did that. We will have to be aware of our surroundings and make good decisions."

Annabella nodded. "I agree. We know the balloons can't hurt us, but those balloons bouncing in the wind can make unexpected moves."

In today's competitive trial, balloons were filled with helium and then tied to rocks, tree branches, and fence rails. They were in the path of the riders. Annabella and Mozart's team would need to walk through and around the balloons without touching them or jumping from being touched by them.

"The judges are watching," Mozart said.

Annabella guided Mozart forward, and Mozart worked with his teammate to get past the balloons with perfect calm.

"I am trying hard not to touch them, Annabella," Mozart said.

"I am trying not to touch them either," Annabella responded.

"I know we can do it!" Mozart said.

Once they were through, a balloon burst in the air behind them, and Mozart jumped. Annabella turned to see her little brother pricking the balloon with a pin!

"Pop!" went the balloon, but her little brother was too late with his joke. Annabella and Mozart had already made it through.

The judges were not happy with Annabella's little brother, so they made him sit in the barn until the competition was over. That is what happens when you are mean.

Mozart was named after a famous composer and Annabella is Hebrew / French for "favored grace"

Mozart and Annabella

"In today's contest," Ray-Ray said, "my friend, Bonita, is with her partner, Isabella. Let's see how they do!"

"Bonita, I think the judges want us to walk over to the mailbox," Isabella said. "We have to get close and get the mail."

Isabella was dressed in her beige riding pants and boots. Isabella, like all riders, was wearing her helmet for safety. Bonita, whose name means pretty, and Isabella were beautiful that day for the contest.

"I think I can do this," Bonita said, "but the creaking sound of the mailbox door makes me cringe, as if someone has run their fingernails down the schoolroom chalkboard. The scratchy noise makes my skin crawl."

"I understand," Isabella said.

These were the two words Bonita wanted to hear. Isabella understood Bonita's concerns and was going to respect those concerns.

Isabella came up with a great plan. "Before we go, let's get the oil can," she said. "I can lubricate the hinges so they don't squeak! Then I will get the mail."

"What a great idea," Bonita said. "Let's do this!"

Isabella and Bonita walked up to the mailbox and lubricated the hinges with the oil. Opening the mailbox door slowly, Isabella retrieved the mail as the judges watched. The judges were impressed with Isabella's idea. They rewarded her with high marks for being considerate of her teammate, Bonita. Bonita was able to stand perfectly still and was not afraid of the screeching, scratchy, scary sound of the squeaky door.

"Remember, my friends," Ray-Ray said, "the two most essential words in any language are, 'I understand.'"

Bonita and Isabella

Khawlah's parents named her after a fierce warrior woman. Khawlah fought with a Muslim army in the first century, on horseback, during the Siege of Damascus. Her brother, Zirrar, who was leading the Muslim forces, was wounded and taken prisoner by the Byzantine army. Khawlah accompanied the army and rushed into the Byzantine rearguard all alone. She saved her brother.

"In today's competition," Ray-Ray said, "my friend, Malik, is with her partner, Khawlah. Let's see how they do!"

"Malik, I think we are going to have to walk through the creek," said Khawlah, adjusting her beautiful Arabian riding clothes so they would not get wet. There are ducks in the stream. The ducks are quacking loudly and trying to scare us."

"I can do this," Malik said. "I am a strong Arabian horse, and I am not afraid."

Khawlah, being only ten years old, said, "But what if those ducks are scared of you and try to fly off? I might get knocked off into the creek, and my beautiful riding clothes would get wet."

Malik, being a wise horse, said, "I understand."

These were the two words Khawlah wanted to hear.

"Hold on tight and face your fears, Khawlah," Malik said. "I will protect you."

"Let's do this!" Khawlah said.

Malik and Khawlah walked through the creek. The ducks were quacking, "Get out, get out!"

Malik was careful not to step on the baby ducks and gently nudged them downstream with his nose. Suddenly, one of the mallards [a male duck] took flight and soared right past Khawlah's head. Khawlah was quick to lean over and grab Malik around the neck.

The quacking ducks were left safe in the stream. The judges were impressed with the quick thinking and kindness shown to the duck family and gave the team high marks for their effort.

14

Malik and Khawlah

Hortensia may be considered the first female lawyer in history. She delivered a speech to the Roman Forum in 42 BC.

The Roman Senate wanted to tax 1,400 rich women to raise money for a war. Roman women in ancient times did not have many rights, and they could not defend themselves. Hortensia spoke on behalf of the women, declaring that they should not have to pay for a war they did not start. Her speech worked. The number of women liable for the taxes was reduced to 400, and they paid the same taxes as men.

Vita's partner was named after this great lady of old.

"We do not have competition today," Ray-Ray said. "Therefore, we will practice. My friend, Vita, is with his partner, Hortensia. Let's go watch!"

Vita and Hortensia were in the riding ring practicing. They walked, trotted, cantered, and when they wanted to go fast, they galloped. These are the four gaits of a horse. Each gait is different and goes from slow (walking) to very fast (galloping). Hortensia also practiced getting on and off Vita.

Practice is important. Hortensia, in 42 BC, practiced her speech before she addressed the Roman forum. Ray-Ray reminded his friends that they must practice if they want to be good at what they do and achieve their goals.

Vita and Hortensia

"In today's contest," Ray-Ray said, "my friend, Octavia, is with her partner, Adrianna. Let's see how they do!"

"Octavia, in this competition, you have to stand very still and let me drink this glass of water," Adrianna said.

"But, Adrianna," Octavia said, "your voice is so sweet, and I want to hear you sing! I want to dance around while you sing!"

Adrianna shook her head. "First, we must do our work for the judges, for they are watching us. Then we can play."

Octavia thought for a moment, then agreed. "Okay, we should do our work first, and then we can play."

Octavia stood very still, and Adrianna drank her glass of water. The judges watched intently. In competition, or when riders and their horses are out for a ride, they want to be able to drink water without getting wet, so the horse must stand very still. Working as a team, Octavia and Andriana showed the judges they could work as a team.

Once she was done drinking, Adrianna began to sing. Octavia began to dance, and the judges jumped up and danced, too.

"You should get your work done first," Ray-Ray said. "Then you can play. That is part of making good decisions."

18

Octavia and Adrianna

"In today's competition," said Ray-Ray, "my friend, Zulu, is with her partner, Kadeesha. The name Kadeesha means 'one with an expressive or outgoing nature.' Let's see how they do!"

"Zulu, we have to work as a team to back up into an obstacle course," Kadeesha said.

"Wow, I am looking at the course, and it is challenging," Zulu responded. "We need to go left and right, in and out. This course is going to be tough."

"Life is sometimes tough," Kadeesha said. "But if we work together, we can do it."

Kadeesha knew how to get Zulu to back up. Using her soft voice, gentle hands, kindness, and leadership skills, Kadeesha encouraged Zulu to back up. Kadeesha did this by gently pulling on the reins and saying, "Back." Kadeesha also applied the slightest pressure with her legs.

After months of practice before the competition, Zulu performed well for the judges, with excellent results. The judges gasped with approval and admired their teamwork. Left and right they went, over the obstacles, around the barn, all the time backing up. Zulu couldn't see where he was going, but he trusted his partner to lead the way to success.

Zulu and Kadeesha

"In today's trial," Ray-Ray said, "my friend, Fusang, is with her partner, An. The name An means 'peace.' Let's see how they do!"

"Fusang, it looks as if we need to jump this fence," An said.

Fusang looked at the fence and said, "That is a mighty tall fence, An. Do you think we can do this?"

"Yes, we can, my friend," An said. "We have done this many times before."

"Yes, I know," Fusang replied, "but not in competition. I am a little nervous."

An got down off her mount and looked Fusang in the eye. "My dearest friend," she said, "be at peace with yourself and believe. Your name represents the tree of life, and what is life without doing our best?"

Fusang thought for a moment and smiled. "I can do this," he said, feeling triumphant.

An got back into her saddle, and Fusang took off, cantering down the lane to the fence. Closer and closer they got. Fusang leaped and cleared the fence with ease. An knew what to say to encourage Fusang, for she knew how to apply the wisdom of the great Chinese warrior, Sun Tzu: "Treat your horses as you would your own family, and they will follow you across the tallest fences."

Fusang is the mythological tree
of life, known to have grown
in the far east of China.

Fusang and An

"In today's competition," Ray-Ray said, "my friend, Taipa, is with her partner, Catori. The name Catori means 'spirit.' Let's see how they do!"

"It looks as if someone has left the gate open," Catori said. "The judges are looking the other way, and if we don't act, some of the other farm animals might get out."

"But if we leave to close the gate," Taipa said, "we will not be able to finish the competition. What should we do?"

Catori thought for a moment, then said, "If someone does not close that gate, Mr. Sheep and his family will get out. If they get out, they could get hurt."

"If we leave to help others, we will lose the competition," Taipa said. "Do you want to give up on what we have worked so hard to achieve?"

Catori nodded. "Yes, it is the right thing to do. The safety of others comes first, and we must act to help others when we can."

Taipa agreed with Catori. They took off, galloping across the fields to close the gate. Mr. Sheep and his family were getting closer to the entrance, unaware of the other side's dangers. Catori saw the cars racing up and down the highway on the other side of the gate and encouraged Taipa to run faster. As Catori and Taipa galloped across the fields, the judges stopped and turned to see what all the commotion was about. All the other riders stopped to watch as well.

Catori and Taipa reached the gate, and from her mount, Catori reached over to close it while Taipa stood very still. Taipa warned Mr. Sheep not to come any closer. Mr. Sheep, realizing the danger of the cars on the other side of the fence, told his family to turn around and go back.

"The grass is not always greener on the other side," Mr. Sheep advised his family. "We need to stay here."

Mr. Sheep thanked Taipa, and then he and his family moved back toward the barn.

As Catori and Taipa walked back, they felt bad, knowing they had lost the competition.

Taipa and Catori

When they got back to the barn, the judges and all the other girls and horses were waiting for them. All at once, the judges began clapping, and then all the other girls began to clap, too. Adrianna started singing with her sweet voice. Catori and Taipa did not know what to think.

The lead judge, Mr. Ansel, whose name means "protector," stopped and asked everyone to listen. "I have never seen such a great ride in all my life," he told Catori and Tapia. "You rode hard, saved lives, and closed that gate from a still mount. We have just witnessed the best trial of the day. It is my honor to award Catori and Taipa with this first-place trophy. Catori and Taipa did what was right for others and disregarded their own well-being."

Everyone applauded and congratulated the team on a job well done.

Moral of the story: Ray-Ray and his friends have ridden with girls from all over the world. This ride is an excellent competition known as life. These girls showed all of us that we need not be afraid. We can achieve magnificent goals if we believe. With faith, hope, and charity, these great teams, working together, believing in each other, can achieve great things.

Catori and Taipa, along with their friends, showed us how to spread our wings. They taught us to believe in the spirit of love for one another.

CPSIA information can be obtained
at www.ICGtesting.com
Printed in the USA
LVHW070358140222
711065LV00006B/142